an Anthology

Sara Dwyer • Patrick Dwyer
Editors

Illustrated and Designed
by Patrick Dwyer

Ice House Press
Seattle

I H P
Ice House Press
Seattle USA

ISBN-13: 978-0692312278
ISBN-10: 0692312277

Cover Photo Credit:
Brinn Cody Dwyer

Printed in the USA

home

Introduction

Sara Dwyer

This is a crowd sourced exploration of home, filtered through language and human experience—disparate paths that heart and voice create. These short works move like dancers in canon: synchronized, simultaneous, augmented and diminished.

To begin, the physical structure within which one lives. A shelter. Downstage, an environment offering security and happiness. Refuge, origin. Entering contrapuntally, the third in our triad of discovery: source, the native and eternal dwelling place of the soul. On the downbeat the deepest current of loss, nostalgia weaving sweetly throughout.

Amidst these symbolic interpretations, we are individual but also the same.

Enter here. An intimate space, a sense of place.

Structure

Doors

Sarah Hunter

White doors. I don't know why they are all white – but they are. Inside and out. Behind each one is where our souls live. The biggest door, the front door, protects all of us. The smaller doors inside make cozy spaces for each of us. We can be together, or a little apart, but still a family.

The doors open and close allowing the ebb and flow of our energy—expanding outside, shrinking back inside. The doors permit us to welcome others to our sacred spaces, our hearths, our hearts.

Home Is

Charlie Sheldon

What you grow into, see, your world, all you know. What is familiar, known, or thought to be known because it is all you know. The air, the trees, the rocks, the weather. The stories, legends, myths. How you learned you got there - moved, brought home from the hospital, sent to. Your world, the paths and lanes, the streams, the glens, the vistas, the dark secret places, the forbidden places. A place imprinted on your fabric of self so you always know it, wherever you are, and you can always return, in your mind, in your self. After years, even a lifetime, it is as if you never left. That is home.

Home

Elaine Douglas

When I started writing about "home" I was overtaken by the feeling I had as a teenager. Yearning for one place. Wishing I had two parents who were together and who lived in one place -- where they still lived and where I would feel a sense of permanency. I thought I was going to write about the different houses we lived in and how I finally realized that "home" was a concept and not a place. And, actually, I had a great experience with "home".

But as I wrote, a troubled, 20-something boy came out. He became a criminal because of the absence of a home. And he never came to acceptance.

I was surprised, but let him come out.

I guess he is part of me. The evil piece of my unconscious that never came to acceptance of what I didn't have.

What this startling event showed me is that "home" is an emotionally powerful concept. It pervades our culture with its expectations. And it can damage us -- particularly those of us whose experience with "home" was different from the norm. It also gave me a deeper understanding of my daughter's anger that we haven't had one home, that her parents got divorced, that she has lived in many houses.

Damn right, she is angry.

Source

Arrival

Lyn Coffin

He had to work late. His car wouldn't start at first. The traffic was a bear. The radio was a mix of static and advertisements. He forgot to get soy milk at the market and had to go back. He had to wait to pay. He didn't have change. There was no room in the garage and no parking space near the building. It was cold. He could only find one glove. The only mail was junk mail. His downstairs neighbor said someone had been taking her paper. Someone had tracked on the staircase.

And then he opened the door and stepped inside and closed the door behind him and turned on the light. And the sign over the fireplace said "You have arrived. You are home." And he knew this referred to a Buddhist text about dwelling in the ultimate. But it was true anyway.

He was home.

Taxi

Mariana Jasso

As soon as I open the taxi door I can smell the house. It is a musky odor, similar to old wood and antique furniture. It has a slight hint of jasmine from my mother's scented oils and a slighter hint of dog urine.

I walk up the stone steps to the front door. The sun shines brighter here. The color of the walls looks almost white. I open the door and the smell is even stronger. I am bombarded by images of the five of us - coming home from summer vacation, coming home from the ranch, coming home from my grandparents' odorless apartment.

As I walk through the door towards the living room I can't find the smell anymore. I try, but it is gone, as always. All I smell now is the rice steaming in the kitchen.

Home Forgotten

Charlie Sheldon

There was a stream here. I remember it. When I was nine my sister and I made a dam, a big dam, a pool, deep. I saw fish there. The stream ran through the fields to the river down back. Our house was there, on that rise. I think.

Dammit. The road hasn't changed but the stream is gone, and those fields are now apartments. Where did the neighborhood go? What happened? I know the new highway cut off the fields, but this, this looks like a city.

When I was a boy this was the country, farms, tobacco barns, potato fields. All gone. It's as if I had no childhood. At least the foreign students here have a home to return to.

This was my home. Now gone. Forgotten. I have not forgotten. I will soon be forgotten. Not even a memory, then.

That dam was something. It flooded the road by the next morning. We got in serious trouble. The police chief lectured us. Then a year later he shot himself for helping himself to cigarettes in Bate's Store. That's forgotten, too. I hope the fish from the stream got to the river before the stream was destroyed.

Where was the neighborhood? It was a mistake coming here. This was not my home. How could it be?

New York

David Snider

ducks serenade melting snow sculptures
the streets reek of pizza
an old couple catches rays on a metal bench
by the fifty-ninth street bridge
the woman from Namibia
smiles, hands me her camera, would you
take my picture with the UN headquarters behind me
framed within the arc of sycamore limbs
I'd be happy to
now the two art-deco skyscrapers form
a backdrop above the children
soaring on their swings
three blocks later I pause on a quiet corner
thirty-fifth and Lexington
two-bedroom apartment for rent (with enormous closets)
this is where I would live, if I could: in the center

Discovery

Motherhood in Outer Space
finding home
Lauryth Orion Johns

At times, being a mom feels so far out. I mean far, far out. Unrecognizable. Scary. Dark.

Like a space ship, rustling from star to star, a lost leaf in the solar winds. Or an orphan exo planet, cut loose from it's sun of origin, drifting.

When things are tough, the bottom drops out of my tummy. I'm falling. The screaming, anxious, wet, ecstatic mess of it just puts me into orbit.

And then there's this feeling, these tiny defenseless people need me, all day, every day. Mine will be the voice they hear when they talk to themselves in their heads, forever. What will I be saying? The pressure becomes so enormous I must be nearing some kind of event horizon preface to oblivion. But no, another day dawns.

It would be easy to lose myself, get lost in the dark parenting space between stars, but that's not the point.

Some one told me recently that hope takes courage. That you have to be brave to think that things will get better. Despite the obvious.

So I unfurl my solar sails (didn't know I had those, did I). Reach out tenuous feelers for the slightest hint of cohesion and light. Turn my rudder and sail towards the warmth of a distant sun.

There's beauty out here too. A daughter's quiet, drooly, sleeping face is a nebula of possibility. How many suns will be born in her, and set free in the universe?

My older girl's laughter as she runs into the sun. So bright. A super nova of color, smell, and sound. Leaving an after image, burning on my heart.

It is right that these things are far apart, with space and darkness in between. Their suddenness is breath taking, the experience intense.

* * *

It turns out, home wasn't where I thought it would be. Not safe and quiet. Planet Earth. Gravity would make this too easy. Ha! No, motherhood is a wandering starship. Beautiful, and difficult to steer.

I've found my home in the galaxies, between the stars. The possibilities are endless, impossible to plan for.

I'm getting comfortable with this feeling. I'm not falling, I'm flying.

And I'm gonna teach my daughters to be starfarers too.

See you out there.

Over the Bow

Patrick Dwyer

The weather did not look good as my brother and sister and I scrambled out the door to pile into the family wagon. We had driven in it, fighting for space, half way across the country to get here, so we all knew our seats now and there was no more squabble about who got the windows. Finally, today, we were going to visit the site of the old farm that we had lived on before we moved East, the place where we had been little kids.

Well, not actually visit, more like look at. And, yes, look at, but pretty much with our imagination. The old farm had been in a steep-sided, deep dell or valley that years ago had been dammed up to make a lake. So we were going to stop and look out across that lake, and down, hundreds of feet down, to where the old farmhouse had stood, to where the creek had flowed across the east pasture, to where Denny and I had played tag with the bull. So, no, we weren't going to see anything but water, but my memory could dive down to those depths and there I would see where I had begun.

The sky got steadily darker as we drove out of Springfield. The note of adventure on which we started out dropped a couple octaves to a sustained basso more suitable to the dubious prospects of family fun ahead of us as we drove down a rain spattered high crown road. Nearing the chain of small lakes formed by the dam, Dad stopped to consult a map and compare it with directions he had once known well. At least, before some of the connecting roads went underwater.

"This way," he told Mom, showing her his map with a finger on a route, "this one follows what we called the old high road, and it just skirts the edge of the valley I think we lived in." Three eager faces rubbered up over the seat backs to try and peer down at this mythical high road on the map's surface. Mom shooed us back so Dad could see better and we started off again, taking the next left fork. The rain got serious.

With rivulets of water pouring down from the crown of the highway into troughs taking up both shoulders, we drove slowly ahead looking for signs that might be familiar to Dad. They talked and pointed to this side and that, but without any apparent certainty, and with not a word of recognition. The old windshield wipers were not doing a very good job now of keeping the windows clear, and the view out the side windows was distorted with a hundred streams of water pouring off the roof and being blown by winds that were rising in force. When the car passed over a high spot, we could feel the wind lift us, just a little, and edge us a sideways. We looked warily at each other but kept our thoughts, or fears, to ourselves.

Dad had told us all a story years ago from when he had been on a troop ship bound for home after the war. There was a part of the voyage where the seas got very rough, and many men made that part of the trip 'on the rails,' as Dad put it, meaning, he added, that they were very sick and hung over the rails so as not to soil the decks. And they could not be coaxed back inside, even though the waves broke over the bow and soaked them all to the skin in very chilly water, and the winds harried their already blanched complexions to the consistency of candle wax.

Then a really big wave, one the sailors called 'a green one,' washed up over the bow as if the boat had finished its tour on the surface and was now diving to the deeps, never to breathe air again. Dad said it was a miracle no one was washed overboard, for when the bow surfaced, all the GIs were still there, though by this time, they looked like so much wet laundry just flung on the rails. Dad always told this as a funny story. It had sounded funny to us, anyway.

Dad told Mom we must be very close now, just as a sharp gust of wind slammed into the side of the car and the car hopped obediently sideways. Another gust and Dad fought the wheel for control, just as a great gray wall of water fell on us. The rain had become suddenly so thick, it was as if it too were a wave breaking over the hood of our car, our bow.

We could see nothing. Even the light, gray as it had been, now went almost completely dark. And there was a sense of movement to the side. Were we floating?

It seemed many minutes that we were suspended like that, in the dark, under water for all we knew. Dad had put on the brakes as best he could. We were stopped, waiting. The squall passed as quickly as it had hit us, the light returned to gray, though it seemed quite bright by comparison. And then the rain let up entirely. Dad told us to stay in the car while he opened his door and peeked out. We obeyed at first, but could not stay in when he set foot outside, and we all piled out. To find ourselves on the shoulder of the opposite side of the road, our left tires only two feet from the rim of the lake. And not a solitary tree between us and the waters covering our old farm.

New Mexico

David Snider

a rainbow flares above the dumpy house
and lights up pear
blossoms like snow
eighty acres of dilapidated outbuildings
rusted tractors and trash
a house modeled after a trailer
yet I hardly notice,
enchanted by lightning above
white sands below
and pine and juniper
right here

Refuge

His House Burning

Peter Wise

Clumps of neighbors in heavy coats stare up at the flames. An old man stands alone in flannel pajamas and slippers, a gray blanket hung across slack shoulders, face lined, skin drooping under his eyes.

"Sally woke me," he says, indicating the dog with a gentle pull of the leash. "She always sleeps on the bed beside me. Pawed my shoulder. Smoke everywhere. Not the smell of burning wood; the stink of the man-made. Wiring I think."

"Couldn't find the little mutt, Tabitha. She sleeps on a pillow next to the radiator. Missing. We had to run."

The upstairs rooms are filling with black lengths of charred attic timbers. The golden retriever stares at the house. She's old, muzzle completely white, as if she just lifted it from a bowl of cream.

We flinch as the remaining first-story glass blows out from the heat. Then a handful of beams crash down and the ground-floor room on the left lights up with sparks and fire.

"The dining room. We had wonderful Thanksgivings - 20, 25 people. Later on, we moved the big table out so my Rhoda could sleep there. Couldn't use the stairs anymore. Three years with the downstairs curtains closed.

"Up in flames. Rhoda's delicate African violets. I just finished trimming the blooms this morning. My stamp collection. Antique tools. Family photos of course; isn't that what everyone cries over when a house burns? I just want the little mutt back."

A fireman tells us to move up the block; the whole house will be coming down. The man with the dog shakes his head.

"Well, at least my niece won't find the letters. I always worried about that. Rhoda's sister and I wrote each other three, four, sometimes five times a year. A private thing. She'd mail them to my office. We said everything in them. God, those were letters."

Fierce crackling and muted crashes as the house begins to fall in on itself.

"I found mine to her when we cleaned out the apartment. Hidden in the bottom of her underwear drawer. Put them in a shoebox down in the basement. Rhoda never knew."

He stops talking and we stare at the house.

"What will you do now?" I ask.

"Go away," says the man.

The front porch of the house falls forward, and then the rest of the structure slowly follows. I retreat as the burning intensifies, leaving behind the old man's silhouette against the flames.

Arizona

David Snider

the river thunders over the vermillion cliff
and loosens into
a thousand ephemeral jewels
that drift, suspended,
and drop into travertine pools,
turquoise ponds
that run one into another
beneath willows and cottonwoods
whispering sweet somethings
in breeze-eeze

Aftermath

Peter Wise

I went home and sat down next to Judy on the deck. Side-by-side, we stared out at the garden together. We didn't say a word.

After about 15 minutes, my phone buzzed. I excused myself and went inside. I stood in front of the kitchen counter, looking at her, my boss on the phone. As we talked, I began assembling the ingredients for dinner. I was concerned about my wife. I blamed her mother, no, that whole family of hers, for, well I wasn't sure for what. For Judy's raging paranoia, and this new phase of conjugal listlessness.

I dug around in the refrigerator and decided to stick to the basics: barbecued chicken and a salad. I lay the chicken breasts out on a cutting board and beat them flat with a fifth of whiskey.   J u d y glanced over when she heard the pounding, but quickly swung her head back toward the garden. I thought of Tammy and wondered what she was eating tonight. From the phone wedged between my cheek and shoulder, I heard the distant sound of my boss's voice.

I glanced outside again and noticed Judy wasn't in her chair. She was standing by the fence, looking over it. I dimmed the lights in the kitchen so I could see better what she was up to.

The phone call lasted almost half an hour. After I hung up, I went outside to light the grill and found Judy back in her chair. I asked her who she'd been talking to.

"Just seeing what was over there," she said.

"And what was over there?" I asked.

"Our neighbor, the man from Shanghai. He was in his hot tub. He had a drink with a paper parasol in it."

"Maybe we should get one," I said. "A hot tub, I mean. Something nice for us to relax in when I get home from work."

"Maybe we should go next door and introduce ourselves," she said. "Maybe he'd invite us over to use his."

We went inside and ate dinner. I thought about Tammy. Judy stared down into her plate, as if gazing at life on the other side of the world.

Loss

My Home the Homeless
Cherry Tigris

My home
no place in particular
the place where throw away people live

My home, a wasteland of broken promises
of waiting and wanting
for something more or less

My home is not a dream come true
or a fairy tale ending
made to pluck at your strings

I am my home
a mood born to me
from man-made hunger

I am the living homeless.

The Sadness of Spring

Anne Herman

Why would a person feel sad in spring, early spring, the time of greatest possibility in the whole year and my new favorite month? February, when everything is budding, nothing has bloomed yet, and it all lies ahead of us. Baby animals appearing. Flowering trees, snowdrops and tulips and daffodils and lilacs... Even the crocuses are yet to come, never mind the moment when the tight red buds on the ends of the tree branches crack open to unfurl tiny, tender green miracles.

Found hyacinths for three bucks today. Among all the bright and blooming pink and white and indigo with the sweet, sweet smell, I chose the tight green buds with just a hint of pink. I choose possibility over actuality every time.

That can leave you empty-handed, though, all the possibility in the future or in my mind, and I don't want my mind to be full and my hands empty. Quite the opposite.

Take dancing. A hand in mine, an arm across my back, legs entwined sometimes, torsos pressed together, belly to belly and heart to heart and music all around us. Multiply that by a whole room full of dancers.

And what about the elk babies? Saw them as I drove home after dancing last night, my first sighting of the year. A newly formed gang of almost-yearlings kicked out by their moms to make room for the new babies. Or maybe they left on their own because their parents were too stupid and embarrassing to tolerate any longer.

So there they are in the road at midnight, a dozen or so babies about four feet tall, looking young and bewildered. Usually I don't see them 'til March or April, and by then they are chasing each other and kicking, and I picture them with spray paint cans like human teenagers.

Sadness in elk babies? Well maybe it's knowing that after these will come another batch next year and the year after that. Time goes on and babies grow up and what is young will always become old.

Me, too.

I used to believe that old people had always been old and I would always be young, but lately it's clear that's not so.

Ran into my old friend Patrick today, my doctor thirty years ago, and as we talked I sensed him looking at me as I was at him. How has time changed you? The lines in your face, the circles around your eyes... What lies behind those? Where have you been and what has happened to you in all this time? What have you done and caused, and what is there still to do while we still have time?

There it is, the sadness again. While we still can...

Yes, it is spring and there are baby animals and sweet pink flowers starting and... And Joan is ninety-one and for the first time ever today she made no sense on the phone. Asked me what those things are you make and hang on the wall, and after a few guesses it turns out it's photographs. She couldn't remember the word.

I am determined never to get old like that, never to be filled with drugs and cared for by sweet Korean women who paint my nails frosted pink whether I like it or not, and then wheel me to sit in front of the TV. I hate nail polish and I hate TV.

Can I avoid ever being ninety-one? God, I hope so.

So Patrick and I talked about a community east of the mountains, of a vineyard and goats and a fig orchard, and how much better it would be to grow old on figs and goat cheese and wine. A lovely vision, a new possibility with an old friend.

Why would possibility make me sad?

Two answers. One is the relentless pull toward actuality, 'cause unless what's possible becomes real in some form, it never was truly possible. Possibility grows into actuality as surely as hyacinth buds open and baby elk grow up. And actuality has limits, disadvantages, stuff you must deal with; you can't just bask in the glow of the future. Actuality is now, and now is both demanding and fleeting.

Not a bad answer, number one, but then there's number two.

My friend Chris says he saw a nightclub hypnotist do a demo one time. He put a guy under and gave him a post-hypnotic suggestion. When you wake up you'll remember nothing, but when I snap my fingers you'll take the umbrella from its stand and open it. Then you'll give a reasonable and coherent explanation for why you did that. You will have a reason.

The guy wakes up, opens the umbrella on cue, and then tells the audience exactly why he did it, with great conviction. The story of human existence.

When Chris does something random he says, "And that's why I opened the umbrella."

Brilliant.

So why am I sad on a soft and bright spring day doing what I love and surrounded by people I respect? Maybe it's because elk babies and buds and old friends add up on this day to the passing of time, and what is sadder than that? Everything growing and blooming, then withering and dying, never to return.

And that's why I opened the umbrella.

Origin

New Mexico 2

David Snider

hiking up the whitewater river
on a bed of maple and aspen leaves
this sunny April day
face caressed by the breeze
and the sweet scent of rotting leaves
stopping to make a fire
six days from here to the Gila
where you'll come out, half-starved yet happy
so you better walk slow, compadre,
with your eyes
and heart
open
the whole way

Smoke Rising

Patrick Dwyer

A chilly night's darkness yields slowly to a graying dawn. Light in the high and narrow east-facing cabin window is already at work. I throw off the thick down cover and slide my longjohns over the edge of the cot as I sit up, appreciate the cold. New snow last night, or more ice, seems likely. Willa is already up, chunking a big piece of hard coal into the center of the remains of last night's banked embers. A thick, reassuring scent of burned coal wafts back to me and foretells a solid warmth for the rest of this cold day. The scuttle grinds on the fieldstone hearth beneath the stove as she slides it over to load bitumen around the anthracite nucleus of this new fire.

"I'll make the tea, if you make the biscuits," I call from the back.

"You can make the tea and the biscuits!" she rejoins. "Earn your keep!"

And my keep here is plenty. Air blown from frosty ridges over the high plains to the doorstep of this Front Range cabin restores my sense of smell, clears ancient fogs from my thoughts. Sleep in a cold room is dreamless. Nothing is served here that isn't whole and there is lots of it. And friendship deep and abiding.

The cabin door bangs on its high-tension spring as she goes out to the shed to refill the scuttle for this evening. The draft of invigorating cold from the top of the world curls around the wool of my socked feet, swirls to freshen the night's air, settles to the sound of the heavy iron stove ticking, as the embers bequeath their last heat to the new blaze and a red glow begins to seep from the isinglass slots in the door.

I light the gas stove under the south window, one burner for tea, the oven for the biscuits, and take out bowl and spoon.

Looking out the ice-rimed window across the snow to the chimney of the nearest neighbor cabin, maybe 300 yards away, my thoughts travel even further, to a smoke filled mountain valley in the Austrian Vorarlburg. To a tiny upper room in a home where Edith and I are guests of an old couple who welcome strangers to make ends meet and also for company. To them we are *fremden*.

Breakfast is black coffee and a small baked bread roll twisted in the rising so it tears easily into wedges when it is served, usually with a pat of ice cold butter on the side. And they are fresh every day. The smell of the baking is still redolent in the kitchen where we sit, with our hosts and our coffee, talking about where to ski today, and the doings of this little village Tschagguns that has been home to this family for hundreds of years.

When our hosts leave for their daily errands, the draft of the morning's outside cold swirls in and around our slippered feet and brings with it the heady scent of the sulfurous coal used in this valley. There really is nothing quite like it, an inseparable part of the sustaining surge of warmth radiating from the green tiles of the stove between the kitchen and the parlor.

This morning, I am drinking an aged and fermented Chinese Pu-erh that comes from the slopes of a remote valley carrying the waters of the Black River, near the top of the world. The smoky taste of the morning's first sip drops me in front of that winter cabin stove, seats me at the kitchen hearth in Tschagguns, palpable scent of burning coal rising over the ice to bring a new day of warmth.

SAFETY
(a Deposit Box)
Leland Roloff

I really must get a safety-deposit box
by noon, tomorrow.
     Then sun high
and bright, I will put some dark parts
into a box.

    Turning in the key,
And nodding to the greyed lady,
I'll put some old contracts away,
Debts you might say,
That were never paid in full.
And, a little jewelry.

"Are you the sole depositor?
The crone mumbles.
      "Quite."
All falls into the box and keys click.
"Is that all?" she asks, wisping away
stray hairs.
      "All."
    And up and out
Of vaults into a one o'clock day.

[Past noon, you might say,
a bit cooler, a change of season
in early fall.
    I can bank on this.]

Rich

Sara Dwyer

It's early morning on the 15th of February. Michael, his lady Emily and I are arranged comfortably in his living room enjoying grower Champagne, slutty Napa Chardonnay and good conversation. He has a bunch of books I like on his walls, authors I'm reading or want to. Good tunes and no personal computer. We talk about these arrangements, easily meandering in words and bubbles.

We've enjoyed Seattle lately, new restaurants and one block neighborhoods popping up like chanterelles in November. We talk rising rents and boutique organic markets and eventually the topic arrives at that old compound noun, the Seattle Chill.

Emily and I, born here, are firm believers. Michael, unconvinced. Of course, Mike can and does charm for a living. It's a little tough to put a word to, but here are a few. A local will smile at you and ask you how you are in the check-out line at PCC, but never invite you home for dinner. Sweet, but unmoved. Of course, who's local now.

Parts of an hour go by unheeded and debate dissolves into one more glass and The Story of How We Met. At first, we don't hear the knocking on the door. On the fifth attempt, Michael answers while Emily and I sit on the couch bemoaning the sensitive hearing of the downstairs neighbor. A minute of undertone conversation and we hear, 'Well, thanks!"

This is not the neighbor. Arriving at the door in time to see Michael, with three long stem red roses and a bottle of Prosecco in hand and a shy smiling man attempting to escape down the hall. It appears he's overheard our earlier conversation and wanted to do his part to show a little seasonal warmth. A rose for each voice he overheard.

There is much shaking of hands, and thanking from all receiving parties. His name is Rich, and he turns down our offer to partake. He was just leaving, he says. Anyways.

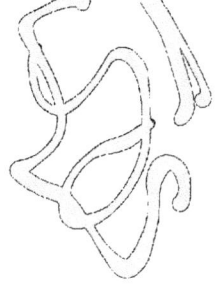

Dwelling

Home Away

Lauryth Orion Johns

Hop. Hop. Jump.

Hop. Hop. Jump.

Emmy scuffed her feet on the path as she walked. She was stalling, she knew. She was already late to school, and mama would be angry to get another note from teacher about her tardiness.

'You left on time. How could it possibly take an hour to walk to school?' Mama would say with an exasperated sigh. She would push Emmy's limp hair out of her face, and give that look. The look that said she hardly recognized the little creature before her, and certainly didn't know what to do with it.

Ever since they moved, it had been this way. Emmy was slow to make new friends, she missed her old ones. Sometimes it felt to her like she couldn't breathe. That the air here was somehow thinner here. Emmy knew that was silly, it was just different is all.

It was hard for her mama too, she knew. A new job, new routines. The isolation was hard, and they only had each other.

Maybe today, she would try to talk to the little black haired girl with the pigtails in her class. The one who smiled shyly at her when they sang in music class. Mama was working so hard, Emmy should at least try to adjust.

She stopped walking and turned to look behind her. Red hills rolled away. Strangely flat and steep at the same time. The dust from her scuffing hung like a trail in the air. She knew it would take a long time to settle.

Even terraformed, the planet's red dirt showed through everything. Add the red grass, grey shrubs, wispy trailing brown trees, and it all gave the impression of bleak crimson desert.

Emmy let her breath out in a huff and pushed her hair off of her face again. She resolved again to do better, make less trouble for her mama. If they could make it here, they could probably make it anywhere. They'd have to do with a lot less when they left on the colony ship next year.

Emmy turned and started to run towards school, her momentum sending her ten feet for every stride she took. She relished the little breeze this speed earned her. Ya, she thought, I could get used to this.

Summers Home

Susan Janko Summers

I

Everything appears small. After remaining so large in my mind the past thirty years, it surprises. Except the trees. Norway maples on either side of the driveway, one for each child, have grown over 60 feet tall. Seven years of living Christmas trees planted each spring when the ground thawed, now congregate in a grove in the far corner of the lot, next to the privet hedge.

It's pretty. Welcoming. The maples reach over the driveway and hold hands. I reach back for a day among the years of days in that home that did not menace, or drag indeterminately, when I was not worried or distracted or longing for anything else but what there was. And what was there? A white clapboard bungalow, a patch of lawn, two maple trees, a copse of distant Christmases. A husband, and a wife. Two children. Things that felt so overwhelming, really so small.

II

"Home is the place where, when you have to go there, they have to take you in."

Or something like that. It moves me when I hear it, but what if you don't want to get taken in? Even there? If when you enter the front door, everything you ever done enters with you, and sits there in the room, and every goddamn person in the room, they steal a glance at you, then look away. They don't have to say a word. Everyone's thinking the same thing. One more kid in CPS. Another of the kids' fathers in jail. One more job lost. One more DUI. What's the point, anyway, going there, if your home's in Russia? It might as well be in Russia.

III

I honestly don't remember that much unhappiness in our home. My siblings insist there were nightly arguments, threats, accusations, recriminations. Bitterness about bad loans to family members. The business lost. Eventually the home.

Did I know this the last summer when I cleared my room of all possessions? Painted the plaster walls a uniform ivory and polished the parquet floors. Moved a single bed frame and mattress back in and situated it in the corner, covered it with a simple cotton drape. Placed a small dresser at the bed's end, void of decoration. The rest of the room empty. Still.

I spent long hours in the room's quiet that last summer. If there was something else in the house, perhaps I closed the door to it. I honestly don't remember.

Away from Home

Sarah Hunter

I'm an ocean away from my house, a stranger, but my mind and heart recognize this place. The pub is around the corner, the coffee shop is on my left. Street lamps march along the cobbled street, leading me up the hill to the place where I know there is an ancient castle. Everything is where it should be. The smell of this place is true and it has been real for me before – I just don't know when. Have I lived here in this life or do I remember this place from a previous existence? As I gaze around and soak in this new, old place I settle, and stay.

Golan Heights

Patrick Dwyer

So much talk tonight about the Golan Heights. She wanted to leave this talk. And the man she was with too. Take her cane and leave by herself, step outside in the company of her own thoughts. So earnest, him, and them. Like any of them knew anything. She could hear it across the many plates of quiet dinner, disparate conversations across candlelit table linens punctuated by the staccato rattle of forks on china. Bringing to her mind the actual sounds of not-so distant battle on those same Heights. *Distant for her now only in the time separating her from that valley of sound then. And that distance, sliding away to nothing ... .*

She slid feet first through the opening between the jagged sandbag walls into the confines of the CP. Down a little dip, too little, it would likely turn out, and under the comically thin roof of post-shored dirt-on-tin that was the roof over this place. Slid, caught herself on the butt of her weapon and caromed back up to a crouch to wait to be noticed by the ant-like occupants of this hole, as they scurried dim-lit from table to table, carrying corrections to the latest map of disaster they maintained here. A grim tale made distant from the battle outside the moment she came to her feet, stumbling a little.

She waited, rifle at the port, suddenly as irrelevant to the proceedings here as they most certainly were to the fighting and dying outside that she had just come in from. The noise of dueling artillery that had surrounded her just minutes ago like the breath of a lover was all now suddenly so distant, as to be only background ambience for dining in one of the exclusive but crowded bistros back in Tel Aviv.

She was out of her element here, as surely as any of these men would be out of theirs, should any of them ever set boot from under this flimsy roof. This was not going well. And as she looked at the disarray of movement, the shuffle of heavy papers, the stink of fear filling this little place, she knew it was only going to get worse.

Her message could wait, would wait. Unimportant now. Curling away in her mind like smoke, even as she stood, crouched. Unnoticed. Was there something running down her leg? Something sticky in her boot, between her toes?

The noises outside fade further, the jangle and drone of alarms and command inside the bunker fade too. She drifts.

A sea breeze riffles her hair, bringing with it the salty hot Mediterranean smells of summer on the Tayelet.

There is laughter with her youngest sister in their home on the Florentin's Uriel da Costa.

Now her friends are calling her to leave her work at the flower market on Yom Tov to come and play. She shakes her curls and tells them they know better - she has a date this evening with … .

The blast of a near-miss artillery round shakes the bunker, ripping to shreds her reverie, her dreams gone to ash like the dust sifting down around her. Leaving only shards of her innocent ideas of home, her assumptions about safety.

Someone is talking to her, has touched her sleeve. A man with a white bandage on his arm helps her to lie on the dirt floor, takes off her helmet, relieves her of her rifle. She suddenly feels very cold.

They tell her she is to leave, right now. Just like that. They are sending her to the rear, to a field hospital, then home. She is confused. What has happened? She'd been sent to the CP with an urgent message. What was the message? Gone.

I can never go home, she thinks. Not now. Not from all this. I could go to my mother and my brothers and sisters and grab them all in an embrace from which only death could pry my arms, my fingers. But it would not be home, she thinks. Not for her.

Ever.

Big Sur

David Snider

it's a long drop
from this boulder
to the ocean's reckless embrace
through sunlight, fog, and spray, but
I'm falling for
that horizon of endless possibility, so
I embrace
my new dark-haired friend
this smiling goddess, draped in sea wrack,
reaching for my hand

www.ingramcontent.com/pod-product-compliance
Lightning Source LLC
Chambersburg PA
CBHW082227140626
46556CB00020B/3386